The Lady's Chair and the Ottoman

NOEL TENNYSON

LOTHROP, LEE & SHEPARD BOOKS   NEW YORK

The copyright notice and Cataloging in Publication information are to be found on the last page.

It was one of those rooms, all flowery and soft, like the kind grandmothers have, and in one corner, under a south window, there was a chair. It was a high-backed wing chair called a lady's chair.

It had a graceful tapered back. Its seat was set on legs that ended in neatly carved feet, and its cover was sprinkled with the leaves of the chinaberry tree.

The lady's chair belonged to Mrs. Seddi Hopewell. It was her favorite chair, the one she read in and did her knitting in, and the one in which she had her afternoon tea. Every evening she smoothed it out and plumped up its cushion so it would look just as nice the following day.

In the next room were a set of armchairs and an ottoman. The armchairs were heavy, overstuffed pieces of furniture. They looked as though fat men who spilled crumbs and smoked cigars had sat in them for years and years. The ottoman was a small footstool set on little brass wheels and covered with the same red velvet as the armchairs. It was placed at the foot of one of the armchairs, where it served as a support for tired feet.

The ottoman wasn't happy. He had never felt he belonged with the two sluggish armchairs.

"They are so dull and slow," he thought, "and I know they really don't like me at all."

The ottoman spent most of his time hoping he would be rearranged. He would have settled for almost anywhere except where he was, but the parlor held a particular attraction for him. Looking through its doorway, he could just see the lady's chair sitting in her corner.

For as long as he could remember, the ottoman had been trying to get closer to the lady's chair. He didn't know why; it was just a feeling that he had.

"Oh, if only I could move," he thought. "If only I could get a little closer to the lady's chair, then maybe I would be happy." It was a difficult task the ottoman had undertaken. Furniture is not supposed to move by itself. Nonetheless, he continued to try.

The overstuffed armchairs were jealous of the graceful lady's chair and snubbed her constantly.

"Why, who does she think she is, sitting there all by herself and not looking like anything else at all?" they sniffed. "She doesn't go with a sofa or even have an ottoman. She's one of a kind, an oddity."

"She's a lot finer than you two tubs," snapped the ottoman, who had just failed in his latest attempt to move himself. He had persuaded a group of house mice to try towing him with bits of thread and string they had collected from Seddi Hopewell's pantry. But the string broke, the mice quarreled, and he was still in the same spot.

Unable to move by himself, the ottoman had to depend on chance opportunities to get from one place to another. Just last week Mrs. Hopewell had had a fit of rearranging. She pushed and pulled the furniture all over the room.

"Over here, or over here?" she muttered, as she moved the ottoman from one place to another. "Oh, my goodness no, that won't do at all," she sighed, for the ottoman's red velvet cover just didn't go with anything but the two armchairs. It was back to them that he was finally returned.

The closest the ottoman had ever gotten to the lady's chair was when a door-to-door vacuum-cleaner salesman tripped over him. The salesman was showing Mrs. Hopewell how nicely his vacuum worked when he stumbled over the ottoman, spilling his entire bag of demonstration dirt in the fall. The ottoman was sent rolling clear across the room to the parlor doorway. But he was quickly replaced by the embarrassed and besmudged salesman, who left him, once again, at the foot of one of the overstuffed armchairs.

For the ottoman, one day ran into another, marked only by dustings and sweepings. His attempts to move himself into the next room continued to be unsuccessful.

"How I wish I had someone to talk to," he thought on his loneliest days. His nearest neighbor was a cherry side table. Her only interests seemed to be checking her polish and wondering if the day would be a moist or dry one. There was a secretary next to her, but the ottoman considered him a snoop because he was always taking notes. The ottoman's only real friend was the grandfather clock. He had just woken himself up by tolling the hour.

"Ahhhhwwwaaa…umm…such a nice nap." The clock yawned in a flurry of clicks and dings as he checked his time. "What have you been up to, Ottoman? Are you still here? Why do I always expect you to be somewhere else when I wake up?"

"Because I've been misplaced," sighed the ottoman. "I know it, I feel it. What am I to do? I don't belong here, I belong with the lady's chair."

"Still trying to change yourself around, are you?" said the clock, adjusting his minute hand. "Relax, Ottoman, or you'll pop your tacks. There's a lot to be said for being part of a complete set—security and dependability, you know. Settle down, watch the dust accumulate, and be happy where you are."

But the ottoman didn't feel complete. He felt like a birthday cake with nine candles on a tenth birthday, or a roller skate with three wheels.

"Perhaps Mrs. Hopewell is thinking of changing the carpet," he thought, trying to stir up a bit of hope. "In that case, we'll all be moved around."

The clock tolled again, and it was time for tea. Mrs. Hopewell was having guests. Soon there was the clinking of teacups on saucers. The birdlike chatter of elderly ladies talking between scones and cucumber sandwiches fluttered in from the parlor.

The prospect of Mrs. Hopewell changing the carpet had the ottoman absorbed in all the possibilities of where he might end up. He was wondering what one corner would be like, as opposed to another, when there was a loud CRASH! All the furniture leaned toward the parlor door to see what had happened. On the floor was a broken saucer, its teacup sitting forlornly on the tea table.

When the tea set was replaced in its cabinet, the widowed cup swung sadly back and forth above the space where its saucer should have been.

While the rest of the room was mourning the loss of the saucer, the two overstuffed armchairs were being selfish, as usual. They tried to divert attention to themselves by ignoring the importance of the event.

"I don't know what all the fuss is about," said one of the armchairs in a superior tone. "After all, tea sets come and go. It's a small loss."

"A small loss?" growled the grandfather clock. "What do you mean, a small loss?" Being a grandfather clock, he had strong feelings about families, and the tea set had just lost a member of its family.

"Well, it's just one saucer. I mean, one saucer isn't much," sniffed the armchair, puffing himself up defensively.

"Today a saucer, tomorrow a cup, and then who knows what's next, maybe the teapot!" said the clock angrily. "There's no end to it once it gets started. Pretty soon you're talking about an incomplete set. It's all downhill from there."

"It's still a small loss," insisted the stubborn armchair. "Insignificant from the larger point of view," he said, puffing himself up even more.

"What nonsense!" cried the infuriated clock. "Insignificant indeed! That tea set has a history longer than all your threads combined. Think of all the happy birthday parties and Christmas mornings that have become part of that saucer. Just consider the comfort it has provided lonely ladies sipping tea together over rum buns and crumpets. How can you not be moved by the loss of such a precious piece of china?"

"Very easily," snickered the armchair, nudging its partner at the idea that any of them might move themselves voluntarily.

"You have no sense of history, no sense of family," charged the clock. "That is quite clear, judging by the way you treat your ottoman."

Not wanting his own difficulties to become the subject of argument, the ottoman quickly changed the direction of the conversation.

"What happens to the parts of sets that get broken or left alone?" he asked, with a certain sense of concern for the lady's chair. She was, as his armchairs had pointed out, all alone.

"Haven't you ever heard of junk shops and knickknack stores? That's where they end up, in sloppy rows of abandoned dining room chairs and lonely crystal goblets, under signs that say ANTIQUES and BRIC-A-BRAC! Take heed, Ottoman," warned the clock. "You may not like your armchairs, but they allow you a certain position you can be sure of." With that, the clock drifted back into himself for another nap. Discouraged and dissatisfied, the ottoman turned to the comforting sight of the lady's chair in the next room.

There's often hope when there appears to be none, and Seddi Hopewell was able to fix the broken saucer. Soon it was returned to its place under its teacup. Everyone was delighted, of course—especially the matronly teapot.

The ottoman would have gone on gazing wistfully at the lady's chair and hoping to be rearranged, except for a turn of fate that ended up rearranging the entire household.

Mrs. Hopewell became ill and went to live with her daughter. Someone came in occasionally and dusted and swept, but she never brushed the ottoman's velvet cover or plumped up the cushion on the lady's chair. Soon it became clear that Mrs. Hopewell was not coming back. The house was sold, and all of the furniture was put up for auction.

It wasn't long before the ottoman and his two armchairs found themselves crowded onto an auction stage. On the other side of the stage the ottoman saw the lady's chair. She was a good bargain for anyone who knew good furniture, and she was one of the first pieces to be sold.

"Going, going, *gone!*" barked the auctioneer, pointing to the lady's chair. A family by the name of Pudney, consisting of Mr. and Mrs. Pudney and three small boys, came to collect their purchase.

The overstuffed armchairs were straining to sit up smartly on their sagging springs. They badgered the ottoman to look his sturdiest in order to attract a good buyer.

"It's a matter of appearance, Ottoman," they prodded. "We can't guarantee you a place with us if you don't measure up." This only made the ottoman droop a little lower on his wheels. Parting company with the armchairs was just what he wanted.

Now that the lady's chair had been sold, the ottoman realized he might never see her again. Despite the grandfather clock's warning, he was determined to follow her in any way that he could, even if it meant leaving the security of his armchairs. And sure enough, his refusal to cooperate resulted in their separation. The armchairs were bought by a representative from a retirement home, who couldn't see much value in the sulking ottoman. The ottoman was sold to one Lawson Cogswell of Cogswell's Grocery.

Mr. Cogswell claimed his purchase and trundled out of the door with the ottoman tucked under his arm. The last thing the ottoman saw, as he was carried away, was the lady's chair being loaded into the Pudneys' station wagon. There were three small boys bouncing and tumbling around her. The car door closed, and then they were gone.

While the Pudneys certainly weren't bad people, they were the type of people who use things up and buy new ones, instead of taking care of things and keeping them forever and ever.

The lady's chair was jumped on and bounced on. The cats sharpened their claws on her, the dog slept on her, and the three small boys played cowboys and Indians on top of her. Very soon she began to fall apart.

The cover of chinaberry leaves became torn, and tufts of stuffing floated out into the room. She was covered with cat hair. Her legs had become wobbly from so much bouncing.

One day, the boys had a great make-believe battle.

"YEE, haaa…" yelled one boy.

"YOWweee!" screamed another, and they collided on their battlefield in a tumbling ball of arms and legs. The lady's chair just couldn't take any more. Her legs collapsed, toppling the boys to the floor. There she lay like a raggedy old shipwreck.

The thin veil of time and history that covered the lady's chair was of no value to the Pudneys.

"There's no sense in keeping a broken chair," said Mr. and Mrs. Pudney when they saw the crumpled piece of furniture. "We'll just buy a new one." They carried her from the house to the back alley and threw her into a pile of rubbish, with all the other used-up things waiting to be hauled away to the local dump.

With no roof to protect her, the lady's chair was quickly soaked with rain. A wet mattress was piled on top of her. Rats scurried about, stealing bits of her tufting for their nests.

One day a particularly large rat was about to nibble at one of her legs when suddenly the mattress was pulled away. Someone picked up the lady's chair, put her into the back of a truck, and drove away into the spring sunshine.

The ottoman was glad to be free of his armchairs, but he had paid a high price for his freedom. By leaving his armchairs, he had lost his security. He was on his own. He was used by Mr. Cogswell as a low bench on which to stand. The ottoman was made for resting one's feet, not for being stood on. He had a hard time standing up under his new job. What's more, his wheels had been removed, which robbed him of his only means of mobility.

He was shuttled all about the grocery store during business hours, but there was a particular nook in which he was put at the end of the day. This he shared with a stepladder and a packing crate. They were used for the same purpose the ottoman was, as something to stand on. Unlike the ottoman, they were well suited for the job. They had no trouble supporting Mr. Cogswell's bulk. In fact, the ottoman made them feel quite superior when they noticed the trouble he was having.

"You know, Ottoman, you really ought to have some rungs and braces like mine," suggested the stepladder one night. "All that fancy stuff only gets in the way," he pointed out, making fun of the ottoman's velvet cover and decorative legs.

"Better still," poked the packing crate, "get rid of those legs altogether, and you'll really be squared away." They laughed at the joke, and at the image of the ottoman sitting legless on his four corners. Losing his wheels was bad enough, thought the ottoman, but losing his legs would be unbearable.

"I used to live in a grand house with velvet armchairs and a beautiful lady's chair," snapped the ottoman in his own defense. "Ladders and boxes were kept in the basement with all the other common service items."

"Oh, you lived in a fine house with a lady's chair," they chided. "Then what are you doing in the back of a grocery store with muddy footprints on your velvet cover?"

The ottoman was about to return the insult when Lawson Cogswell opened the store and whisked him away to change a light bulb. The grocer hoisted himself onto the tired footstool. Reaching for the light bulb, Mr. Cogswell tipped the ottoman onto one side, teetering dangerously. Feeling the hopelessness of his situation, the ottoman thought longingly of the lady's chair and wondered if he would ever find her again. He felt lost and homesick. With the strain of the grocer's weight threatening to destroy him completely, the ottoman took a chance. Hoping to save himself, he pivoted slightly on a corner leg, just enough to set Mr. Cogswell off balance. He felt the grocer's weight shift. There was a sharp CRACK! One of the ottoman's legs snapped right off. The grocer toppled into a stack of Cocoa Crinkles and Sugar Dinkies.

"That's it," he sputtered, picking himself up. "That's it for you, Ottoman!" And he put the ottoman under his arm, went out the door and down the street, and sold him to a used-furniture store for five dollars.

Hardly aware that he had been sold, the ottoman tried hard to balance on his three remaining legs. He was tired and worn out. The pile of his red velvet cover was crushed and dirty.

He found himself sitting in a room filled with furniture. There was a sofa without a seat, a table without a top, and all kinds of chairs in various states of disrepair.

"Oh no!" thought the ottoman nervously. He remembered what the grandfather clock had said about junk shops and knickknack stores. "Could this be one of those places? Perhaps I should have listened to the clock and not been so brash."

The ottoman was convinced that he was in a junk shop. What would life be like? One dusty day after another, surrounded by ill-used furniture, suffering from loose joints and old paint. "How will I survive?" he thought in panic. "There's nothing meaner than an empty chest of drawers." And he imagined a tall bureau backing him into a corner.

"Ottoman! Hey, Ottoman! Are you all right?" called a voice, bringing the ottoman back to reality. He looked up to see a pretty loveseat. "You look like you need a lift," she said, noticing the ottoman's missing leg.

"Where am I?" asked the confused ottoman. "This isn't a junk shop, is it?"

"Certainly not!" answered the loveseat, slightly offended. "Do I look like a piece of junk?"

On closer inspection, the ottoman realized that she was a fine Victorian restoration. "Oh no, that's not what I meant at all," apologized the ottoman. "You see, I really don't know where I am."

"You're in Duncan Fiefe's used-furniture store. He's a great fellow, a real artist."

"An artist?" queried the ottoman.

"He can take you apart and put you back together as good as new," said the loveseat.

"Can he fix my broken leg?"

"Absolutely. What's more, he'll welt your seams and dust your cambric. He'll stuff your stuffing, glue your gimp, and then tack you all together. Take that chair, for example," she said, looking behind the ottoman. "Duncan brought her in a few days ago. What a mess, a real bag of bones. But look at her now. If that's not art, then I'm a hideaway bed."

The ottoman had already begun to think he had fallen into good hands. But when he turned to look at the chair behind him, he was suddenly and joyfully convinced of it. For there, closer than she had ever been before—only a few feet away, in fact—was the lady's chair.

The loveseat's admiration for Duncan Fiefe was not unfounded. He was always trying to make used-up things useful again. He even made a point of looking in places where people tend to put their old, worn-out things, like front stoops and back alleys.

He knew what things were worth, and he was quick to take advantage of a good bargain. And a good bargain was what Mr. Cogswell had been carrying when he marched in with the broken ottoman. The grocer didn't know the value of the ottoman, but Duncan did, and he gladly bought it for five dollars.

"This must be my lucky week," he thought. "First I find a beautiful lady's chair in a trash heap. Then a silly grocer sells me a fine ottoman for five dollars."

Duncan looked at the battered ottoman sitting next to the lady's chair. There was a certain familiarity about it, as though he had seen it somewhere before, or had seen something like it at least.

"It's a handsome ottoman," thought Duncan. "Should I keep it or sell it? There's not much of a market for ottomans alone. I'd like to keep it, but I can't keep everything," he reasoned, looking around his crowded workshop.

Nevertheless, no one would be interested in buying a three-legged ottoman with a worn-out cover. So Duncan picked up his tools and went to work.

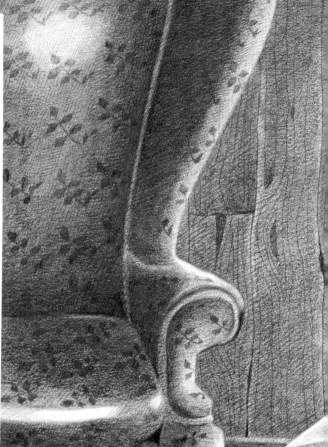

He fixed the ottoman's broken leg, gave him a new set of brass wheels, and polished up his woodwork. All that remained to be done was replacing the velvet cover. He carefully pulled out the tacks that anchored the cover in place. He gave a gentle tug, and the cover dropped onto the floor. Duncan's heart skipped a beat. He looked at the ottoman, then he looked at the lady's chair, and his mouth dropped open in astonishment. For there, beneath the ottoman's red velvet cover, was another cover, the original one. Just like the lady's chair, it was sprinkled with the leaves of the chinaberry tree.

Duncan's astonishment turned into delight. He laughed and laughed at what he considered a wonderful coincidence. Two pieces of matching furniture, each turning up separately by chance—was it just a coincidence? Of course not. The ottoman's reunion with the lady's chair was perfectly understandable. They had been made for each other, and for some whim or reason they had been separated. The ottoman had been covered in red velvet and bound to overstuffed armchairs, and the lady's chair had been left to sit alone.

With the light heart of someone who has just discovered a very special secret, Duncan gave them new, matching covers. At the end of the day, he took them home.

He arranged the lady's chair and the ottoman together in his own parlor. As Duncan was leaving the room, something made him stop and turn around. Perhaps it was the satisfaction he felt from seeing them together, or just the sunny spring day outside, but he knew something had been made right. He felt a spark of happiness inside, and so did the lady's chair and the ottoman.

For my sister Leslie

with special thanks to Rick and Anne Foley

First Edition 1 2 3 4 5 6 7 8 9 10

Library of Congress Cataloging in Publication Data
Tennyson, Noel.   The lady's chair and the ottoman.
Summary: An ottoman has spent as long as he can remember trying to get close to a lady's chair; and though fortune separates them and they seem to come to unhappy ends, a marvelous coincidence reunites them in a very happy way. 1. Children's stories, American. [1. Furniture—Fiction] I. Title.
PZ7.T2642Lad   1987   [E]   84-11196
ISBN 0-688-04097-7   ISBN 0-688-04098-5 (lib. bdg.)